Visit us on the Web! randomhousekids.com

Educators and librarians, for a variety of teaching tools, visit us at RHTeachersLibrarians.com

Library of Congress Cataloging-in-Publication Data
McKeown, Adam (Adam N.)
A Christmas carol / by Charles Dickens; retold for young readers by Adam McKeown ;
illustrated by Gerald Kelley. — First edition.
pages cm.
Summary: A miser learns the true meaning of Christmas
when three ghostly visitors review his past and foretell his future.
ISBN 978-0-553-51199-4 (trade) — ISBN 978-0-375-97463-2 (lib. bdg.) — ISBN 978-0-553-51200-7 (ebook)
[1. Christmas—Fiction. 2. Ghosts—Fiction. 3. Great Britain—History—19th century—Fiction.]
I. Kelley, Gerald, illustrator. II. Dickens, Charles, 1812–1870. Christmas carol. III. Title.
PZ7.1.M45Ch 2015
[E]—dc23
2014029944

The illustrations for this book were created with watercolor and digital media.
Book design by Nicole de las Heras

MANUFACTURED IN CHINA
10 9 8 7 6 5 4 3 2 1
First Edition

CHARLES DICKENS
A Christmas Carol

Retold for young readers by
ADAM McKEOWN

Illustrated by
GERALD KELLEY

Doubleday Books for Young Readers

Jacob Marley was as dead as a doornail.

He died on Christmas Eve and nobody noticed. He was not expected at any Christmas parties. He had not invited anybody to his house. He had no friends and cared for nothing but his money. The only person who went to his funeral, although he did not cry a tear, was his business partner, Ebenezer Scrooge.

Scrooge! Now, he was a hard-hearted, greedy old miser! No winter frost was colder than Scrooge, and no wind blew more bitterly. If he had a heart, it was frozen solid. His hair was white, his lips were blue, and his skin was pale and crackly. He spent his days counting his money, and when each day ended, he walked home alone to an empty house, where he lived as solitary as an oyster. And that's the way he liked it.

It was Christmas Eve, seven years to the day since Marley had died, when Scrooge's nephew, Fred, bounced into the office of Scrooge and Marley with a loud "Merry Christmas!"

"M-m-m-merry Christmas," said Bob Cratchit, Scrooge's clerk, who was shivering at his desk.

"Bah!" said Scrooge with a wave of his hand. "Humbug! Christmas is a humbug! Fred, why are you here?"

"To invite you to Christmas dinner," Fred replied, "and to ask if you would give something to help the poor."

"Help the poor?" asked Scrooge with a nasty laugh. "Are there no prisons? Bah to your *Merry Christmas*! Now, get out of my sight, both of you."

Scrooge left the office and edged his way through crowds of carolers and partygoers, stopping only once to swing his cane at a boy who got in his way to sing, in hopes of a penny. He made his way to his house at the end of a grim, lonely street. It was the saddest and gloomiest house in all of London.

He groped through the darkness for his door, but when he came to the step, he was met by an eerie green light. It was the door knocker! The brass lion's head was gone, and in its place—looking out with unblinking eyes—was the face of Jacob Marley.

Scrooge shuddered and gasped. Marley was dead and had no business staring at him where the door knocker should be. He rubbed his eyes, and the face was gone.

"Humbug," he muttered as he went inside. Scrooge was normally not afraid of the dark. Darkness was cheap, and he liked it. But on this night he took a candle with him as he climbed the stairs to his bedroom. Once there, he chained and bolted the door from the inside. "Humbug!" he said again, annoyed at being fooled by a trick of the light.

But as he was about to blow out the candle, every clock in the house began to chime. There came a sound from deep in the cellar: a heavy chain grinding across the stone floor. Up the cellar steps it came. *Boom!* went the cellar door, flying open. Then there was a *clank!* and a *clump!* on the stairs to Scrooge's bedroom, coming closer and closer until the sound was right outside his door. The flames in the fireplace leapt up, blinding Scrooge for a moment, and when his eyes cleared, there, standing before him, was Jacob Marley.

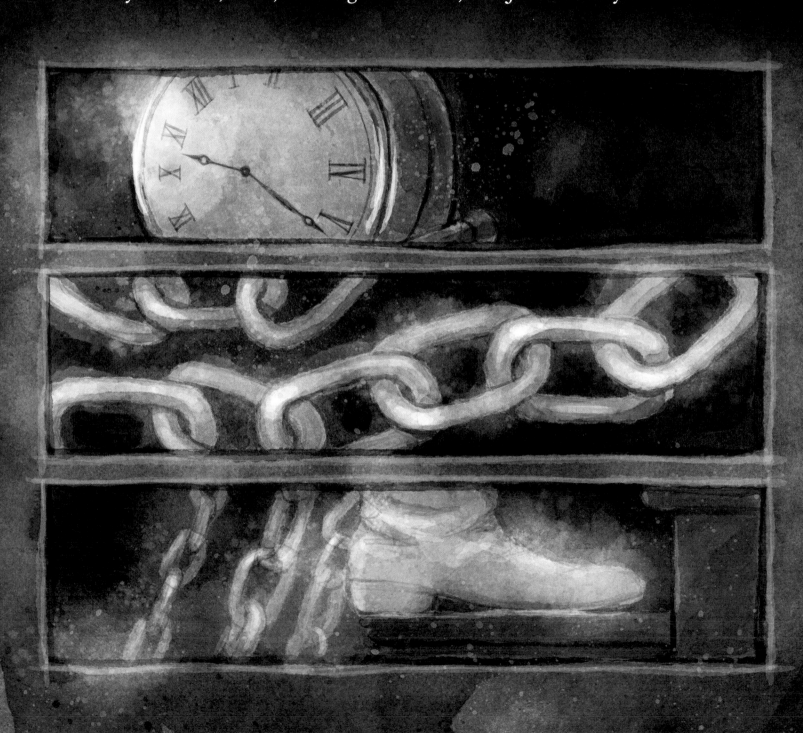

"What do you want with me?" cried Scrooge.

"You will be haunted," said Marley, "by three spirits: the Ghost of Christmas Past, the Ghost of Christmas Present, and the Ghost of Christmas Yet to Come. Expect the first when the clock strikes one."

"Bah!" said Scrooge. "You're nothing more than a bad dream!"

The ghost let out a hideous cry. "Look at my chain!" Scrooge could scarcely keep his eyes off it. It was made of purses, cash boxes, and money bags—all clasped together with iron locks. "I made it in life, link by link and yard by yard, by hoarding money instead of sharing my good fortune. Now I must carry this awful weight forever. Your chain will be even heavier than this one, but you may have time to free yourself."

The ghost vanished.

Scrooge looked around his room. The house was silent. "Humbug," he said, and blew the candle out.

Scrooge awoke in darkness. Had Marley been a dream? Then he remembered his warning: he would be haunted when the clock struck one.

He waited. The minutes seemed long, too long. When finally the clock rang and nothing happened, Scrooge let out a laugh. "One o'clock!" he said. "And nothing! All a dream!"

But then the church bell struck a dull, sad sound and the bedroom was flooded with light. An old man appeared, the size of a child, with long white hair but not a wrinkle on his face. In his hand was a sprig of holly.

"I am the Ghost of Christmas Past," he said in a gentle voice.

"Past?" said Scrooge.

"Yes," said the spirit. "*Your* past. Rise, and walk with me!"

The foggy London streets were gone. In their place were farms and fields. They reminded Scrooge of days and hopes and joys long forgotten.

"I know this place!" said Scrooge. "I was a boy here!"

Scrooge ran down the country road, passing faces he once knew. "Hello!" he cried, but the figures were only shadows of the things that had been, unaware of the visitors from another time.

Next they came to a schoolhouse. Scrooge stopped in his tracks. The joy he had felt a moment before was gone. "In there—" Scrooge stammered.

"Is you," said the spirit. "A child left all alone on Christmas."

"No child should be alone on Christmas," Scrooge said, and a tear fell from his eye. "Yesterday a boy sang to me on the street. I wish I had given him something."

The spirit looked at Scrooge tenderly. "Come," he said. "There is another place you know well."

They suddenly found themselves in an office much like Scrooge's, but brighter and warmer and full of people. A gentleman burst through the door where young Scrooge and another man were working. "No more of that tonight, lads!" he boomed. "Clear these desks and make way for a party!"

"Old Fezziwig," said Scrooge. "Alive again." In came a fiddler, and Scrooge could hardly keep his feet from moving to the music as Fezziwig whirled around the room, stuffing coins into everyone's pockets.

"It takes so little of your money to make people happy," said the spirit.

Scrooge was ashamed of how stingy he had been with Bob Cratchit. "Spirit," he said, "remove me from this place. I do not wish to see more."

"I cannot. These are your own memories of Christmas, which you cannot forget." As he spoke, Scrooge's bedroom slowly came into focus, and the ghost flickered away like coals in a fireplace.

Scrooge sat in darkness alone by his bed. "Humbug!" he growled, then climbed into bed and fell into a deep sleep.

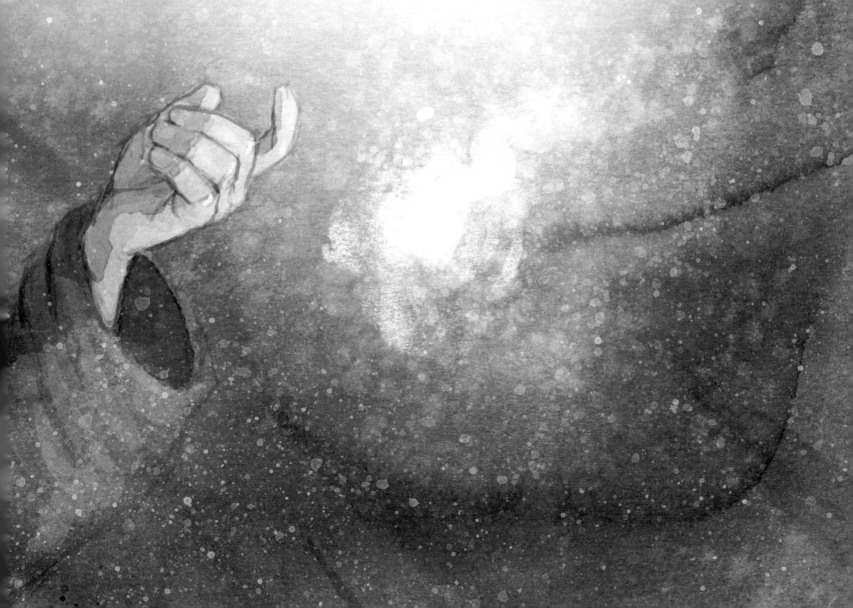

Scrooge awoke in a panic. The room was dark, and he knew the clock was ready to strike one—again.

But nothing happened. Minutes ticked by. Nothing. Scrooge was just about to say *Humbug!* when his bedroom was bathed in golden light. Shading his eyes, he followed the light to the next room.

It was decked from floor to ceiling with ivy, holly, mistletoe, and bright berries. In the midst of it all was a great feast: roasted turkeys and geese, hams and sausages, puddings and pies, cakes and cookies, apples, oranges, and pears! Sitting on top was a giant of a man draped in a green velvet robe, his chestnut-brown hair crowned with a wreath. "I am the Ghost of Christmas Present," said the spirit. "Come closer and touch my robe."

Scrooge did as he was told and found himself flying above the rooftops, looking down on the streets below. Everywhere there was joy and celebration.

Scrooge felt like a fool. There was such happiness on Christmas, even among those who had so little. Why should he, who had so much, be unhappy?

They flew past the windows of houses full of people playing games and feasting. In one, Scrooge saw a face he knew. "It's my nephew, Fred!" he said. "Do you think we could stop here, Spirit?"

But on they sped to the outskirts of the city, where the poor working people lived.

They came to a shabby cottage, too small for the large family sitting down to Christmas Eve dinner. Bob Cratchit came in, and on his shoulders was Tiny Tim, the youngest of his children. He was too weak to walk without a crutch.

The Cratchits had saved all year for a fine goose, which came out of the oven golden brown. Before they ate, Cratchit raised his glass. "Let us drink to the health of Mr. Scrooge, to whom we owe this feast."

All the children groaned—except for Tiny Tim, who lifted his cup in his frail, trembling hands and said, "God bless us, every one!"

Slowly the frowns turned to laughter as the feast began.

"Spirit," pleaded Scrooge, "is there no help for this family?"

"Are there no prisons?" said the spirit.

The church bells started to chime and the ghost began to fade. "If things do not change, the child will die," the spirit said, and the Ghost of Christmas Present vanished into nothing.

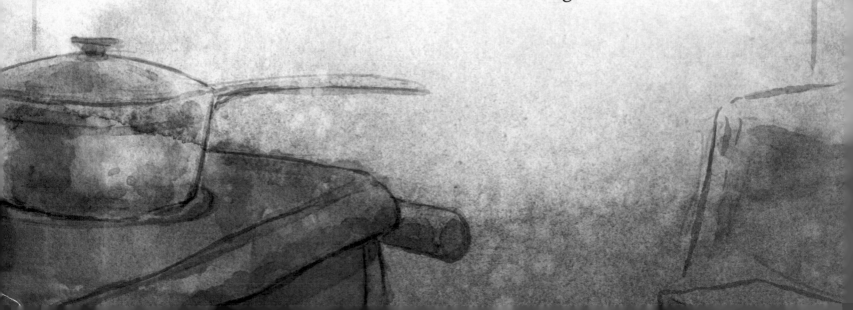

Soon Scrooge saw the third spirit, moving toward him like a mist along the ground.

It was silent, shrouded in a deep black robe, with nothing visible but one pale hand.

"You are the Ghost of Christmas Yet to Come?" said Scrooge, his voice quivering. "You are going to show me things that will be?"

The ghost pointed into the blackness.

"If you will not speak, then I must follow," said Scrooge. "I do not have much time to undo all the misery I have caused."

The ghost led him to a forgotten graveyard. A terror gripped Scrooge. "Spirit," he said, "tell me Tiny Tim is not here in this sad place." The phantom said nothing but merely pointed to a grave.

Slowly Scrooge looked at what the ghost was pointing to.

It was a rough block of dark stone.

It read EBENEZER SCROOGE.

"No, Spirit, no!" cried Scrooge, dropping to his knees. "Why show me these things if I cannot change them? I will change. I will not forget the lessons of Christmas Past, Present, and Future. They will live within me all year long! Tell me I may sponge away the writing on this stone!"

Scrooge grabbed at the spirit's hand—but the black hood collapsed and the Ghost of Christmas Yet to Come was gone.

But there in its place was Scrooge's bed! Scrooge was back home, and he still had time to change his life!

"I am alive!" he cried. "I will wipe away the shadows of what could have been!"

Church bells chimed as Scrooge threw open the window and shouted to a boy on the street. "What day is it today, my fine fellow?"

"Today?" replied the boy, confused. "Why, it's Christmas Day!"

"Then I haven't missed it!" cried Scrooge. He flung fistfuls of money to the boy. "There is a turkey in the market—as big as you. Go buy it and take it to Bob Cratchit's house." Then he threw more coins to the boy, who ran off like a shot.

What a glorious day it was! Scrooge ran down the street, wishing everyone a merry Christmas, until he got to a home he knew well. "I hope they will forgive me," he said, and rapped on the door.

His nephew opened it, looking very surprised, indeed.

"I have come for dinner, Fred," said Scrooge, "if you will have me, and to add some money to your collection for the poor."

"Of course," said Fred, turning to his guests and shouting, "It's my dear uncle Scrooge!"

Scrooge and the family ate and sang and laughed, and when the music began, old Scrooge even danced.

The day after Christmas, Scrooge arrived at his office earlier than usual. At a quarter past nine, the door opened quietly and Bob Cratchit snuck in.

"Cratchit, you're late!" growled Scrooge, pretending to be angry.

"But Christmas is just one day a year, sir," said Cratchit.

"Not anymore!" roared Scrooge. Then his smile broke into a laugh. "Cratchit, I am raising your salary. And I am going to help your family. Now go home to them. You're a good man."

For a moment Cratchit thought Scrooge had lost his mind.

"Merry Christmas, Bob," said Scrooge with a kindness that could not be mistaken.

Scrooge was true to his word. He became a good neighbor, a good citizen, and the dearest friend to Tiny Tim, who grew healthy and strong.

And never again did he meet with any ghosts. He lived in the spirit of Christmas Past, Present, and Future every day of his life.

May the same be said of us all. And so, as Tiny Tim said, God bless us, every one!